# I Gave Thomas Edison My Sandwich

**Floyd C. Moore**

*Pictures by* **Donna Kae Nelson**

Albert Whitman & Company • Morton Grove, Illinois

Dedicated to all my family and friends, and especially
to all children, whose magic day is waiting just down the tracks.  F.C.M.

With love to my dad, Don, and to my mom, Norma.  D.K.N.

Hi! My name is Floyd.  I was born in 1908.
That was a long time ago, before computers or
TV.  We didn't even have a radio!
But still, exciting things happened...

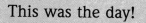

This was the day!

I knew it as soon as my eyes flew open. My feet were over the side of the bed so fast I stepped on my dog, Tater. I threw on my shirt, jumped into my pants, and snapped the galluses over each shoulder.

I hummed as I splashed cold water on my face from the cornflower bowl and combed my hair with my fingers.

"Floyd!" Mother called from the kitchen. "Come and eat your breakfast before the ham gets cold."

I knew then that she remembered, too. She never brought ham out of the smokehouse except on Sundays and special days.

Oh, yes, this was the day!

After a gobbled breakfast of fried mush and ham, I headed for the door.

Mother caught me by the galluses and twirled me around for final inspection. She combed my hair again, this time with *her* fingers. "You be careful of that train, you hear? And mind your manners—not every boy gets to see what you're going to see." She dabbed at the corner of my mouth with the end of her apron. "And remember your Papa wants to hear every last detail when he gets home tonight."

She handed me my lunch pail and kissed my cowlick flat.

"It's souse I packed in your lunch today," she called as I hopped down the steps. "And, yessir, I put mustard on both sides of your biscuit!"

"Thanks, Mother!" I waved over my back. She knew how I loved her homemade lunchmeat called souse, especially if the mustard was so thick the souse would slide like my sled on Hampton hill.

Country ham and souse?

This really *was* the day!

Hurrying down Chinaberry Street, I saw Mr. Eckels sitting in his porch swing. His crutches leaned against Mrs. Eckels's fern box as usual.

"Hey there, Floyd." He waved above the ferns. "Are they gonna let you young 'uns out for the big celebration?"

"Yessir. The whole school's going to the depot."

"Mighty fine. You can shake ole Henry's hand for me." Mr. Eckels chuckled. "He makes a real spiffy car."

I started to tell him I couldn't possibly do that. We fourth graders would probably be buried in the back of the crowd. Instead, I asked if he was coming.

"Nope. My hip's flaring up again. It wouldn't do to get stuck in that crowd. But you stop by and recollect it all for me, okay?"

"Sure will," I called.

Crossing Memorial Street, I thought about Mr. Eckels saying I could shake Henry's hand for him.

Touch Henry Ford? The man who invented the Ford automobile? Impossible.

But I was going to lay eyes on him. Me. Floyd Moore. Fourth Grader, Iron City Grammar School, Iron City, Tennessee. I would actually get to see the man who invented Papa's automobile.

Oh, indeed, this was the day!

Class was just starting as I tossed my lunch pail under my bench and slid in next to Ramey Johnson.

Mr. Stribling tapped his cedar rod against his hand. "Class, let's settle down. We'll be leaving soon, but first I want to review who these famous visitors are."

He turned to the blackboard where three names were printed. They had been there for two weeks. He pointed to the first one:

*William Taft.*

He said each word slowly as though he were tasting every letter.

"William Taft," we repeated, just as slowly.

"And who is William Taft?" Mr. Stribling asked.

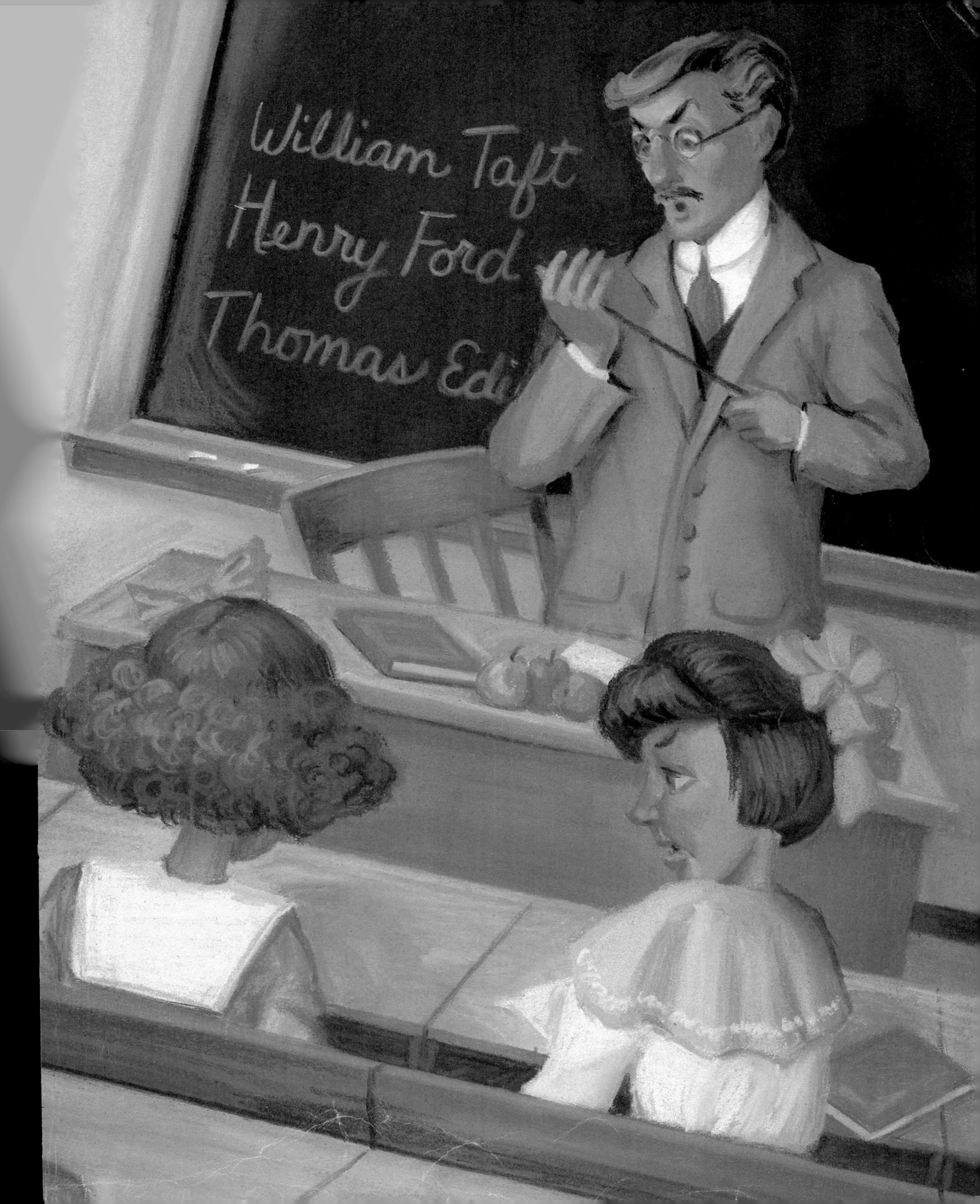
William Taft
Henry Ford
Thomas Edi

Imogene Riley waved her hand so hard she looked as if she was going to shake it off.

"Yes, Imogene?" said Mr. Stribling.

She turned to face the class. "William Taft was the twenty-seventh president of the United States. Woodrow Wilson is president now."

"Exactly." Mr. Stribling beamed. "President Taft was our twenty-seventh president, and Woodrow Wilson is our twenty-eighth."

"I bet Ramey Johnson can't even count to twenty-seven," Imogene hissed as soon as Mr. Stribling had turned to the blackboard. She flicked her tongue out at Ramey.

The whole class hated Imogene because she was so smart and acted like she was the drum and the drumstick, too.

"*Henry Ford,*" Mr. Stribling said slowly.

"Henry Ford," we repeated, just as slowly.

"Henry Ford invented the Model-T automobile," Imogene shouted out before Mr. Stribling could call on anyone else.

Ramey reached in his pocket, then leaned toward the stove. But I grabbed him. He loved to bring marbles, heat them on the stove, and flip them at Imogene's back. Today, though, he could ruin everything. The whole class could be detained, and I was not about to be left behind.

"*Thomas Edison,*" Mr. Stribling was saying, his eyes riveted on Ramey.

"Thomas Edison invented the light bulb," Ramey supplied.

Imogene looked cheated.

"Class?"

"Thomas Edison invented the light bulb," we chanted faintly.

Now we could hear the fifth and sixth graders passing under our window. Oh, boy, we were next!

"Thomas Edison," Mr. Stribling was saying in a voice that threatened one person to move, "invented many useful things, including the light bulb."

Weren't we ever going to be dismissed? The train was due at 9:30, and it was over a mile to the depot!

"He also invented the phonograph, and he improved motion pictures," Imogene added, with her I'm-so-smart smile.

Ramey leaned toward me. "And Imogene Riley invented the big mouth," he whispered.

"All right, class, it's time to go," Mr. Stribling said. He told us to take along our lunches since trains run late, especially celebrity trains. "You realize, I'm sure," he added as he reached for his coat, "that you are about to see three of the most important men in the world. It is something you will tell your grandchildren."

We formed a line and marched toward the square. Ramey kept stepping on Imogene's heels, and she kept jabbing back with her elbow.

By the time we got to the depot, the band was already playing. My worst fear had come true—our class was in the back of the crowd, practically squashed against some grownups.

Imogene complained to Mr. Stribling that she couldn't see.

"It's safer here," he said. "You don't want to be in front of a surging crowd."

My chin drooped onto my cradled lunch pail. I had looked forward all week to viewing these famous Americans, and now all I could see was Mrs. Simpson's bird-of-paradise hat!

But about that time a space opened up, with Constable Walker standing on one side and Deputy Holcomb on the other. They were dividing the crowd with roped partitions.

Hurray!

Then they formed an aisle through the middle of the crowd so that Ramey and I were next to the runway. A ringside seat!

We heard a train whistle. Everyone shouted, "They're here! They're here!"

With labored snorts and groans, the train came into view, then slowed to a heaving stop.

I could see white flags waving from the cowcatcher, but strain as I might, I couldn't stretch tall enough to see anyone in the windows.

Suddenly I got an idea. I sat my lunch pail down and stood on it, bracing myself by holding onto Ramey's shoulder. Now I could see everything.

The conductor swung down the train steps followed by mean-faced men. "They're the guards," Ramey whispered. They scattered through the crowd as the drums began a steady roll.

"There he is!" someone cried as a large man with a moustache stepped down. Cheers went up everywhere. Mayor Briggs came forward and offered his hand. It was trembling slightly.

"Welcome to Iron City, Mr. President."

President Taft smiled, then shook hands with the mayor while nodding to the crowd over the mayor's shoulder.

I had never seen such a bear of a man, and tall as timber to boot. He was even taller than Mayor Briggs.

"Mr. President! Over here!" Ramey and I shouted.

But President Taft was shaking hands with people on the other side of the aisle. He never even turned around.

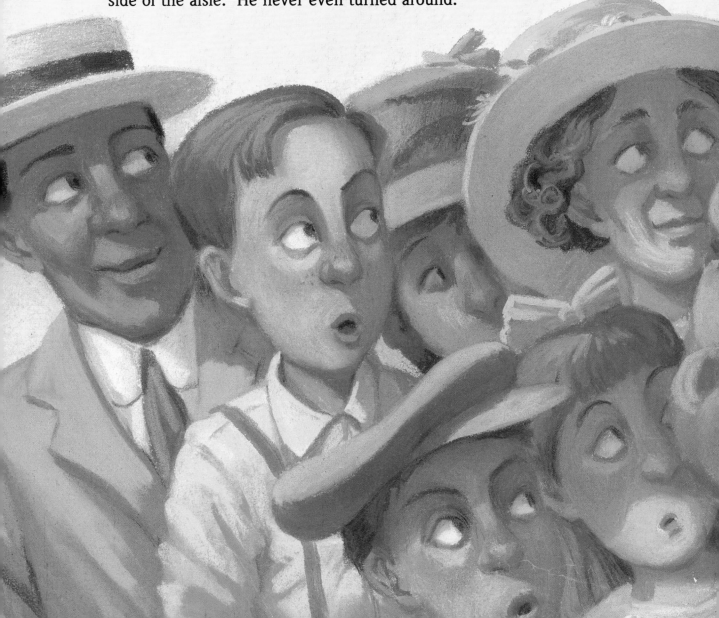

A thin, wiry man came onto the platform. "That's Henry Ford!" someone shouted. Mr. Ford accepted Mayor Briggs's hand briefly, then stepped to the side and waved. His gaze was as sharp as Mr. Eckels's whittlin' knife.

"Oh, no," I groaned. Mr. Ford was not going to come down the runway.

Two celebrities, and neither of them even smiled at me. Was this all I could tell Mother and Papa and Mr. Eckels?

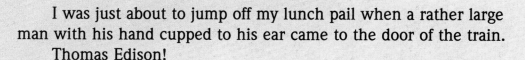

I was just about to jump off my lunch pail when a rather large man with his hand cupped to his ear came to the door of the train.

Thomas Edison!

It had to be. Mr. Stribling said that the famous inventor was hard-of-hearing because a conductor had once pulled him by his ears onto a train platform. He was only twelve years old then.

"Mr. Edison! Mr. Edison!" the crowd called.

He smiled, then started walking directly toward our section.

"He's coming! Oh, Ramey, he's coming!" I shouted, squeezing Ramey's shoulder.

Thomas Edison shook hands along our side, then suddenly halted directly in front of me. My heart stopped.

"And what have we here, son?"

I followed his eyes to my lunch pail. My face was burning. I jumped down. "My lunch, sir. I mean—"

"Is that any way to treat your ham sandwich?" He laughed as he winked at the crowd.

"It's not ham, sir, it's souse—" I caught myself. How dumb! He hadn't come all the way to Iron City to find out what Floyd Moore carried in his lunch pail!

"Souse?" He made the word sound like it was an old friend. Then he held out his hand to me. Not to Ramey or Imogene or Mr. Stribling. To *me*. "I used to eat souse when I was your age. Haven't thought about that in a long time."

"With lots of mustard, too," was all I could think to say as he pumped my hand up and down.

"That makes it even better." His eyes were kinda softlike. "Enjoy your lunch, lad."

W

And with that he moved on down the line.

I had just shaken hands with Thomas Edison, the inventor of the light bulb! My brain squatted on that thought. Ramey was nudging me about something, but I couldn't move.

I don't know how the three men got back in the train or when the constable took down the ropes. I just remember everyone surging forward as the whistle blew.

"Class," Mr. Stribling was shouting, "stand clear of the tracks!"

Then I guess recklessness hit me. Papa always said it ran in the family—Mother's family. Anyway, I simply couldn't let Thomas Edison chug out of my life, so I reached down, pried my lunch pail open, grabbed my souse biscuit still wrapped in Mother's blue dishcloth, and ran over to the conductor.

"Floyd!" I heard Mr. Stribling scream behind me.

"Give this to Mr. Edison," I shouted above the noise of the train as I held my sandwich up. "Tell him it's souse. He'll know."

The conductor took it hesitantly, studied it from all sides like it was a turtle or something, then disappeared into the train.

Then the train disappeared.

I never did find out if Mr. Edison actually ate my sandwich. But you know what? That day has never disappeared from my memory—and it happened over seventy years ago.

Yes, indeed, *that was the day!*

**Floyd C. Moore** was born in 1908 in Lawrenceburg, Tennessee, where he grew up playing sandlot baseball, reading, and attending movie matinees. As an adult, he worked in civil engineering, from Montana to New Mexico to Kentucky. Yet he always found time to write poetry and stories, to act in little theater productions, and to travel.

When Mr. Moore was young, trains carrying celebrities traveled from town to town across America so that people could see and perhaps even talk to famous persons they had only read about in newspapers. One day a celebrity train carrying William Taft, Henry Ford, and Thomas Edison came to Iron City, Tennessee, where Floyd was living. The whole school went down to the station to greet it. When Thomas Edison stepped off, he stopped to talk to Floyd. This story is based on that exciting event.

Floyd now lives in Nashville, Tennessee, with his wife, his daughter, and his beloved black-and-white cat, Mr. Tux.

**Donna Kae Nelson** has worked for several years in children's publications as a designer and illustrator. She attended the American Academy of Art in Chicago and lives in Evanston, Illinois. She has also illustrated *The One and Only Delgado Cheese.*

Moore, Floyd C.
  I gave Thomas Edison my sandwich / written by Floyd C. Moore; illustrated by Donna Kae Nelson.
    p.   cm.
  Summary: A story based on the author's memories of a field trip during which he met the inventor of the light bulb.
  ISBN 0-8075-3504-4
  1. Edison, Thomas A. (Thomas Alva), 1847-1931—Juvenile fiction. [1. Edison, Thomas A. (Thomas Alva), 1847-1931—Fiction.]   I. Nelson, Donna Kae, ill.   II. Title.
  PZ7.M78363Iae   1995                                                                      94-22009
  [Fic]—dc20                                                                                      CIP
                                                                                                 AC

The design is by Karen A. Yops.
The illustration medium is pastel.
The typeface is Weidemann Medium.

Text copyright © 1995 by Floyd C. Moore.
Illustrations copyright © 1995 by Donna Kae Nelson.
Published in 1995 by Albert Whitman & Company, 6340 Oakton Street, Morton Grove, Illinois 60053-2723.
Published simultaneously in Canada by General Publishing, Limited, Toronto.
Printed in the United States of America.
10  9  8  7  6  5  4  3  2  1